HATventures of Hope

Jenny McCray

ISBN: 978-0-9911489-7-4

Printed in the U.S.A.

Book design by Dave Reed
Illustrations by Jessica Donehue

Manufactured by Thomson-Shore, Dexter, MI, USA; RMA596MS687, August, 2014

Dedication

For Lindsay – Your strength and fighting spirit
inspire me beyond words.

I hope for the day that we wear pink for its
beauty rather than for its message.

There's a germy inside of my mommy.
I've been told that its name is "cancer."
But when I ask where cancer came from,
my question receives no answer.

I've heard she and cancer are battling,
and she's putting up quite a fight,
but it's going to take some time
for her doctors to make her all right.

So, my mommy goes to "treatment"
to keep this mean bug away,
and her medicine sure is silly--
it made her hair fall out one day!

Mommy says I can't catch her germs,
so we can hug whenever we please.
And now it's become my duty
to make certain her head doesn't freeze.

She says my job is the biggest,
and I must not let her down.
I choose the hats on her head each day
as we make our way around town.

These hats are so very special.
They take us to magical places.
Each hat brings a different adventure,
as we celebrate each day's graces.

After early morning snuggles,
it's time to get to work.
Racing over to the hat shelf
I grab two with a smirk.

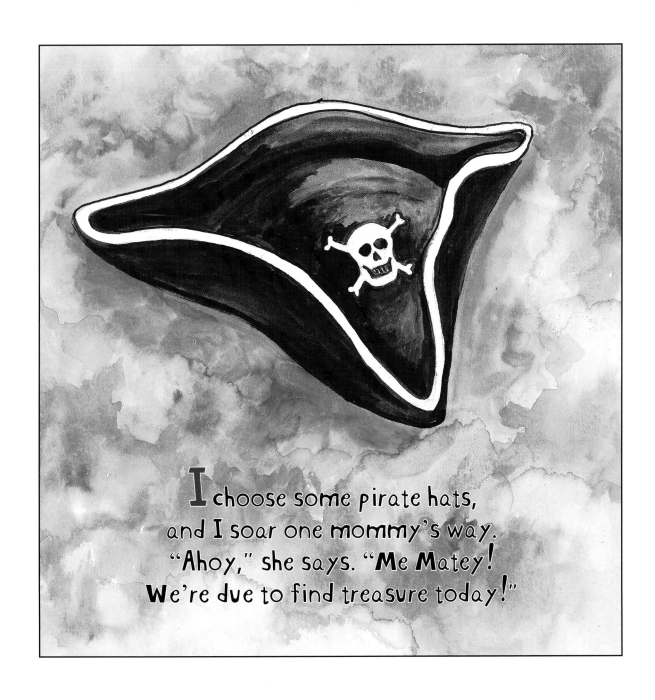

I choose some pirate hats,
and I soar one mommy's way.
"Ahoy," she says. "Me Matey!
We're due to find treasure today!"

Suddenly with a glow in her eyes
and a smile across her lip,
she laughs and leaps high onto the couch,
and it's become our pirate ship.

We set sail through choppy waters -
we brave the stormy weather.
There is nothing that can stop us!
We're our best when we're together!

The waves are splashing beneath us.
A mist lingers upon my face.
I blink the fog from my eyes
as I lean into mommy's embrace.

Then before I can catch my footing,
we discover we're close to land,
and I fall with the jolt of the vessel
as it staggers onto the sand.

We scurry off the ship
running arm in arm,
and quickly set off through the jungle
to find us some pirate charm.

We trudge to the peak of the mountain.
"**X** marks the spot" as they say.
Then together we begin digging
for treasure is not far away!

Faster and faster we're moving
as we don't have time to rest-
CRACK! Hooray! **W**e've found it!
We've hit a treasure chest!

We head back toward the Jolly Roger
and sail home with our lucky find,
but as our journey nears its end,
fresh adventures skip through my mind.

New days bring new chances
for us to conquer and explore.
Today we wear safari hats
as we browse the grocery store.

The aisles become a jungle maze
with animals lurking near;
as we hurry 'round the bakery
I'm met with my worst fear!

Face to face with the jungle king!
He crouches on the prowl.
Mommy pulls me behind the muffins
as we hear the lion growl!

We creep by the donuts,
grab a box for home,
and then tiptoe toward the produce
as the lion starts to roam.

We sneak to the bananas
and quickly snatch a bunch.
The monkeys watch us closely
thinking we'll be jungle lunch.

Rounding another corner,
we dart from the mighty beast.
"Not today!" says mommy,
"Choose someone else for your feast!"

Then just as I catch my breath,
I am frozen with great surprise
staring up at a bulging elephant,
I cannot believe my eyes.

I tip my hat to the giant,
and she swings her trunk in delight.
Then I bid farewell to a giraffe
as our safari ends for the night.

A circus show on Tuesday means
a striped hat two feet tall.
Mommy leads us to our section,
and I know we'll have a ball.

The ringmaster steps into view,
firmly plants his feet in place.
Then the steam pipe music blows,
and my heart begins to race.

"Come one, come all!" he bellows.
"You won't believe what's in store!"
And with two claps of his hands,
firecrackers burst from the floor.

My heart skips a beat for moment.
I can hardly contain my delight.
I look up at mommy with giggles
and squeeze her hand so tight.

The trapeze artists glide through the air
and calculate tricks with precision:
Fluid in every motion,
and mindful of every decision.

Then in one spectacular movement,
while barely making a sound,
they finish their execution
landing safely back on the ground.

Then suddenly out of the shadows
five jolly faces appear.
So full of fun and mischief
that we're grinning from ear to ear.

Into the spotlight they tumble,
flipping in every direction.
Acrobats wild and free,
yet landing stunts with perfection.

They dive through blazing hoops,
and juggle pins covered in flames,
while pulling pranks on each other
playing silly clown games.

In a flash, the clowns are before us,
we're chosen to join their fun.
They lead us onto the floor,
and a new adventure has begun!

I stand proudly with my mommy,
and our laughter has us in stitches
as our new friends circle 'round us,
clowning through dance-like twitches.

Mommy grasps both of my hands;
together we spin round and round.
All the clowns join in the frenzy,
then we collide and fall to the ground.

As we help each other stand
and dust off the dirt from our clothes,
we're still laughing in this moment
that means more than anyone knows.

I know deep down in my heart
it's a memory we'll never forget.
One that we'll keep forever
in a place of no regret.

It's off to the park on Wednesday,
mommy dons her finest crown,
and the playground morphs into a castle
with a water-filled moat wrapped around.

Dressed as an iron clad knight
with a shield across my chest,
I know that my mission is tough,
and my strength will be put to the test.

For mommy has been locked away
high up in the castle's tower
by a very naughty dragon
with fire-breathing power.

I charge toward the palace
waving my sword in hysterics,
blasting through block and stone
destroying the fortress' barracks!

Then rushing across the drawbridge,
my dagger tucked at my side,
I crouch down low to the earth
eying a safe place to hide.

I dart behind some bushes,
hoping I haven't been spotted.
Then I quickly catch my breath
and continue the plan that I've plotted.

Scaling the castle's tower,
I spy the dragon up ahead.
He's firmly standing guard
and now my heart sinks with dread.

But I muster up the nerve
to face the angry brute
and climb the tower wall,
preparing to aim and shoot.

Then suddenly I've been noticed:
there's not a moment to spare!
As he spits his fiery venom,
my dagger shoots through the air!

I successfully hit my target,
the dragon falls to his doom,
and I clamber inside the tower,
to free mommy from her room.

Pounding straight through the door
where mommy waits with affection,
she greets me with a hug
thankful for my protection.

We stay in that hug for a moment
because I never want it to end.
For any time spent with mommy
is time spent with my best friend.

Sombreros to the doctor's
as we conga down the hall.
Raiding and trading on long-ships
in our Viking hats through the mall.

Witch hats on Halloween
on broomsticks flying free.
Firefighter helmets keep us safe
from a blazing fire's debris.

Chef hats in the kitchen
as we host our cooking show.
Cowboy hats on horseback
chasing outlaws on the go.

Astronaut helmets on bike rides
rocket us up into space,
and ball caps at a baseball game
where mommy steals third base.

Our marvelous **HAT**ventures
brighten even the darkest days.
They keep us feeling hopeful
through this cancer journey craze.

And even on a day of rest,
mommy paints it with new meaning,
by showing me time spent together
is more important than how she's feeling.

Mommy's tummy hurts today.
We're resting in her bed.
We snuggle close together
with camouflage hats on our heads.

Because even on a sick day,
imagination still runs free,
and suddenly her bed transforms
to a fort up in a tree.

We cannot move or shiver.
We keep our breathing low.
We lie still as statues
for dinosaurs roam below!!

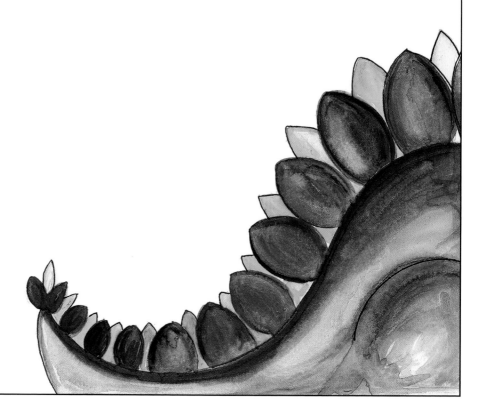

With covers over top us,
neither utters a word.
We nap in our tree house all morning
hoping never to be seen or heard.

Listening to each other breathe
fills the silence of this day,
and no sound is more peaceful:
it's perfection in every way.

Each night is just as special
because as mommy holds me near,
I drift away to my sweet dreams
as she whispers in my ear:

"For you, I'll fight a dragon
or the meanest cowboy in town.
I'll wrestle with a lion
and tango with a clown.

I'll fight for you forever
and always keep you near.
Nothing can come between us--
I love you most, my dear.

I love you bigger than elephants
and taller than giraffes.
I love you more than ice cream
and more than belly laughs.

I love you more than safaris
and any **circus** show,
more than pirate's treasure
or castles **high** and low.

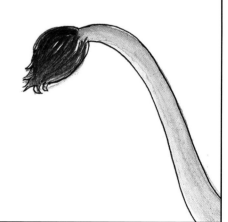

You are the music to this dance,
even when we are apart.
For you aren't the keeper of my head,
but the keeper of my heart."

As I wake up in the morning,
rubbing my sleepy eyes,
I notice Mommy beside me,
and I have one last surprise.

"Come with me, Mommy," I tell her,
and off to the hat shelf we go.
"I have something special to show you,"
but it's only for us to know."

I delicately pick two hats,
knowing she sees nothing there.
Then proceed to unwrap the scarf
that covers her head with no hair.

Mommy lets her scarf unravel,
and I watch it fall to the floor.
I know this crusade is different:
One we haven't conquered before.

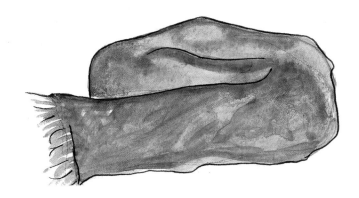

"These hats aren't like the others," I say.
"They're the most unique of their kind.
A product of trust and faith:
they can only be seen with your mind."

"They are invisible hats," I explain.
"And I have just these two,
but you must be brave to wear them,
so I want to wear mine with you."

She wraps her arms around me,
eyes wet with happy tears.
I know a weight has been lifted:
I have helped to calm her fears.

"Thank you, my little hero," she says.
"You make my days so sweet.
These hats are incredibly special:
our collection is complete."

Then we lift our hats together,
as we put them on with great haste.
Both smiling about our secret,
in this moment that can't be replaced.

Mommy never looked so pretty.
These hats are the best of the best.
I feel so very proud
to be the leader of this quest.

Our hats give us the power
to adventure near and far,
but they also give us the courage--
to be just who we are!

After the breast cancer diagnosis of my best friend, Lindsay, at her young age of 28, my eyes were opened to the world of cancer more than ever before. Watching loved ones and strangers alike rally around her as she navigated her way through this unexpected discovery was incredibly inspiring. As destructive as this disease can be, it also has the unique ability to unite people in ways I never thought possible.

Two and a half years after her diagnosis, Lindsay became a mother for the first time via surrogate. Children have such a powerful way of being the light in times of darkness, and the amount of love circulating through the room on the night her son was born was immeasurable. Being moved by her journey, I decided to write a children's book capturing the love between a mother and child through a cancer diagnosis. I also wanted to do something to give back to the cancer community as so many of these warriors have forever touched my life.

As I began to write, I knew immediately that my sister would be the perfect illustrator of this book for more reasons than her artistic talent. Cancer has indirectly touched and affected both our lives through many ways, and it certainly has left an impact on both of us as it has to so many others. She was excited to be a part of this meaningful project, and it was a dream come true collaborating with my other best friend!

Because I am the owner of an in-home daycare, children have always been my passion, and I spend most of my days in the land of imagination. I also enjoy running, reading, writing, taking pictures, chasing after my busy toddler, and spending quality time with family, friends, and my husband.

My sister, Jessica, is a former pediatric nurse turned professional homework helper, play-doh molder, boo-boo healer, chef and chauffeur – or what some call a "stay-at-home" mom. She's certainly the life of every tea party! When she isn't spending time with her husband and three children, you can find her scrapbooking, reading, cooking, snapping pictures, sketching or in a Pilates class.